To Charlotte,

my spirited and creative daughter. You were the spark that ignited my passion for writing and the driving force behind this book. Your boundless energy and imagination inspired me to create a story that would capture the magic of our bedtime story adventures. Your laughter and joy are woven into every page, and I am forever grateful for the gift of creativity you brought into my life. This book is for you, my dear Charlotte, with all my love and admiration. May it inspire you to always chase your dreams and never lose your sense of wonder.

Nosey Nancy Nose Picker

Written by Joe B. Balady

Illustrated by Darlee Urbiztondo

Nosey Nancy was a curious little miss.
She liked to pick her nose all day, with so much bliss.

4

But one day she picked and picked,
And suddenly, her world was flipped.

Picking boogies is no fun,
It turned her into a dragon!

8

That never happened to her before,
But with that last pick, out came a r o a r

She spun around with a great big wail,
Her skin turned scaly from head to tail.

10

She saw her reflection in the mirror,
That scary sight could not be clearer.
Her teeth grew sharp, and her breath was fire,
Her skin was blue as a sapphire.

12

13

But just like the gem, she was also pretty,
She glittered and shined, like the brightest city.

She stumbled, then flew to the highest mountain,
Where she knew of a place with a magical fountain.

She splashed herself with
The fountain's strange water,
Hoping to return to just
Being a daughter.

And just like that, she was herself again,
But something was different, a mystery to mend.

Her nose was clean, and her hands were free,
No more picking for her, as you can see.

10-11-19

21

She was still nosey, as she's known to be,
But not a finger goes up there, "just tissues for me."

Boogie picking was finished, it's over, it's done,
No more picking for her, for she had a good reason.

23

So remember, kids, when you want to pick,
Just use a tissue, it's much more slick.

The story is true, believe all the lore,
For how Nosey Nancy Nose Picker
Became a nose picker no more.

BALADY
BOOKS

Thank you for choosing my book!

Reviews are important for authors. If you enjoyed the story, please take a moment to share your thoughts.

Share the magic of Nosey Nancy Nose Picker with your loved ones! Gift them a copy of the book or share a link to purchase it. And as a special thanks, message me on Instagram with proof of share for a <u>free</u> Nosey Nancy coloring book download. Thank you for being a part of my literary journey and for supporting the creation of more "Magical Stories for Little Minds!"

BALADYBOOKS

ISBN 979-8-9908183-1-6
This book is registered with the Library of Congress under registration number TXu 2-355-744. All rights reserved.

About the Author

Hello there! I'm Joe Balady, the creative mind behind Nosey Nancy Nose Picker, my debut children's book. As an adoptive parent of a curious 5-year-old, I've discovered a newfound passion for writing children's books. With a background in advertising and communications, I've always been drawn to creative storytelling. But it wasn't until my daughter inspired me that I decided to take the leap and publish my first book.

Join me on this exciting journey as I explore the world of children's literature and bring my stories to life. Follow me on Instagram @baladybooks as I share updates along the creative journey for new books in the works!

About the Illustrator

I'm Darlee Urbiztondo, also known as Happylee, a creative artist from the Philippines and sometimes Belgium. I've illustrated 16 children's books and counting. I love working with self-published authors to bring their stories to life and be part of their creative journey. I specialize in digital illustrations, painting, calligraphy, graphic design, and traditional art. My skills in book formatting help authors make their books shine. Art is a big part of who I am, and I aim to create fun and magical pieces that make people happy. My books reflect my heart and soul. I enjoy simple pleasures like coffee, books, movies, TV shows, travel, anime, and singing.

Check my works
www.thehappylee.com

Printed in Great Britain
by Amazon

46618472R00018